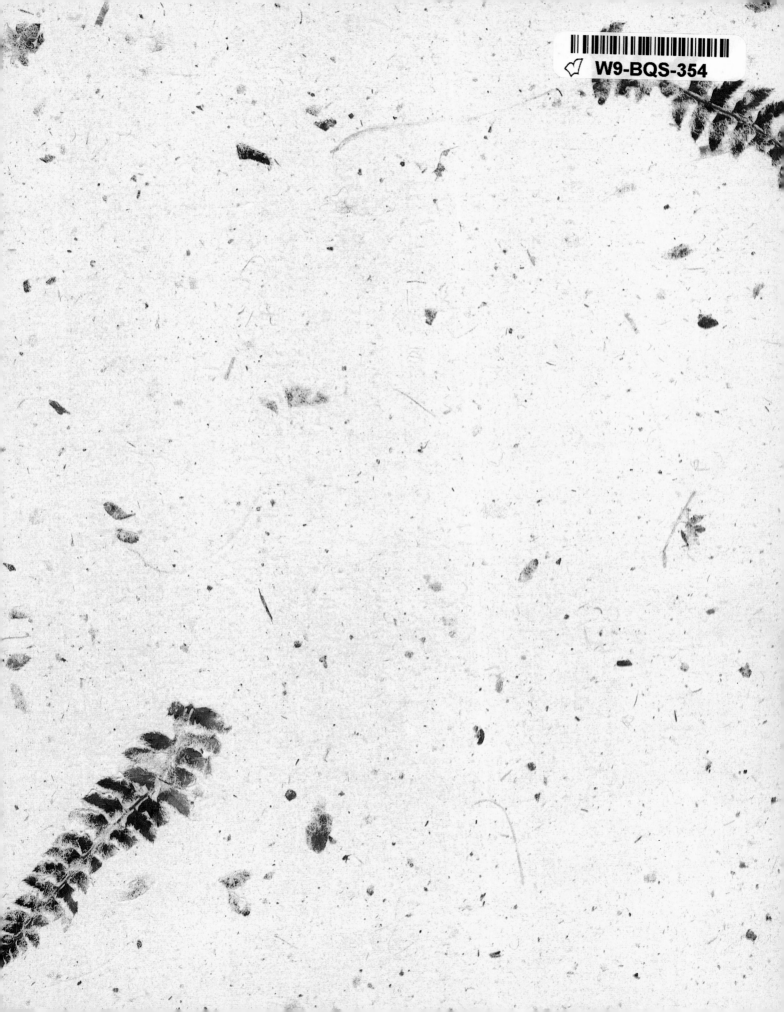

Edited by Belinda Gallagher
Designed by Oxprint Ltd

*The publishers would like to thank Dover Publications Inc. New York for the use of woodcuts from '1800 Woodcuts by Thomas Bewick and his School' from the Dover Pictorial Archive Series, first published in 1962.*

ISBN 0 86112 629 7
© Brimax Books Ltd 1991. All rights reserved
Published by Brimax Books, Newmarket, England 1991.
Printed in Hong Kong

# ÆSOP'S FABLES

Retold by Graeme Kent
Illustrated by Tessa Hamilton

Brimax · Newmarket · England

# CONTENTS

| | |
|---|---|
| The Astronomer | 44 |
| The Bald Huntsman | 47 |
| The Bee-Keeper and the Bees | 52 |
| The Birds, the Beasts and the Bat | 40 |
| The Boasting Traveller | 66 |
| A Boy Bathing | 62 |
| The Boy and the Hazelnuts | 54 |
| The Boy and the Wolf | 26 |
| The Caged Bird and the Bat | 60 |
| The Crab and his Mother | 74 |
| The Crow and the Water Jug | 14 |
| The Dog and his Reflection | 12 |
| The Donkey and his Shadow | 24 |
| The Eagle and the Beetle | 92 |
| The Fisherman and the Sprat | 82 |
| The Fortune Teller | 122 |
| The Fox and the Bramble | 28 |
| The Fox and the Crow | 50 |
| The Fox and the Grapes | 30 |
| The Fox and the Stork | 64 |
| The Gnat and the Bull | 34 |
| The Goatherd and the Goat | 94 |
| The Grasshopper and the Ants | 78 |
| The Greedy Fox | 22 |
| The Hare and the Tortoise | 38 |
| Hercules and the Wagoner | 19 |
| The Horse and his Rider | 46 |
| The Hound and the Hare | 32 |
| The Hound and the Lion | 8 |

| | |
|---|---|
| The Hunter and the Woodman | 48 |
| Jupiter and the Monkey | 100 |
| Jupiter and the Tortoise | 76 |
| The Lamp | 106 |
| The Lark and the Farmer | 58 |
| The Lion and the Mouse | 70 |
| A Man and his Sons | 102 |
| The Man and the Satyr | 80 |
| Mercury and the Woodman | 86 |
| The Mice in Council | 68 |
| The Mice and the Weasels | 118 |
| The Moon and her Mother | 20 |
| The Mouse and the Bull | 10 |
| The North Wind and the Sun | 116 |
| The Oak and the Reeds | 124 |
| The Ox and the Frogs | 104 |
| The Oxen and the Wagon | 18 |
| The Peacock and the Crane | 72 |
| The Pig and the Sheep | 35 |
| The Piping Fisherman | 114 |
| The Quack Frog | 112 |
| The Soldier and his Horse | 98 |
| The Spendthrift and the Swallow | 110 |
| The Stag at the Pool | 84 |
| The Swan and the Crow | 120 |
| The Town Mouse and the Country Mouse | 36 |
| The Traveller and his Dog | 108 |
| The Travellers and the Plane Tree | 42 |
| The Trees and the Axe | 90 |
| The Two Pots | 56 |
| The Wild Boar and the Fox | 31 |
| The Wolf and the Goat | 16 |
| The Wolf and the Horse | 88 |
| A Wolf in Sheep's Clothing | 96 |

# THE HOUND AND THE LION

A hound decided to visit the jungle and see what he could find there. He had never been in the jungle before and did not know many of the animals who lived there. This did not worry him. Where he came from, he had been considered a great hunter. He had chased and killed many animals. He was sure that all the beasts of the jungle would be afraid of him.

Before very long he saw a lion walking ahead of him. This was the first lion the hound had ever seen. The thought did not worry the hound at all. He thought that he would soon catch the great beast.

For a time the hound followed the lion through the jungle. Then he broke into a trot and prepared to leap on the other beast.

Just as he reached the lion, the great animal turned and stared at the hound.

Something warned the hound that the beast he was facing was stronger and fiercer than any he had ever met before.

For a moment the two animals stared at each other. Then the lion opened his mouth and roared.

The hound had never heard such a terrifying sound. The roar echoed among the trees. The hound discovered that he could not move. He stared at the savage teeth of the lion. He noticed the strength in the beast's shoulders. Then the hound turned and ran.

He raced through the jungle as fast as he could go, his heart thumping with fear. He had only one wish, and that was to put as much distance as possible between himself and the animal with the dreadful roar and the frightening teeth.

A fox who had been watching, laughed aloud and called after the vanishing hound, "It didn't take much to make you run, my friend!"

| **Moral** | *We should find out as much as possible about someone before coming into conflict with him.* |

# THE MOUSE AND THE BULL

When it happened, it surprised everyone. A cheeky little mouse went up to a bull as the great animal was grazing. Suddenly the mouse darted forward and bit the great bull on the nose.

The bull roared with surprise and fury. The mouse turned and fled. Lowering his horns the bull charged after the tiny creature.

Just when it looked as if the bull would catch up with the mouse and toss it high into the air, the tiny animal reached its hole in a wall and scuttled in to safety.

The bull snorted and pawed the ground outside the hole, daring the mouse to come out and face him. The mouse laughed at him.

This was too much! The bull backed off and then charged at the wall, butting it with his head. He repeated this several times. The strong wall did not even shake. The bull realised that his head was now very sore. He felt dizzy and sank to his knees.

This was just what the mouse had been waiting for. As the exhausted bull sprawled on the ground, his head only a short distance from the hole, the mouse darted out and bit him on the nose again!

This time the bull's angry roar could be heard all over the fields. He rose to his feet and tried to trample on the mouse. The big animal was far too slow. The mouse was already back in his hole.

The bull bellowed and stamped his feet until the ground shook. There was nothing else he could do.

Presently a little voice squeaked from the safety of the wall, "You big strong fellows don't win all the time, you know!"

| **Moral** | *Size and strength is not always enough.* |

# THE DOG AND HIS REFLECTION

A dog was feeling very proud of himself. He had found a large piece of meat and was carrying it away in his mouth, so that he could eat it in peace somewhere.

He came to a stream and began to cross over a narrow plank which led from one bank to the other. Suddenly he stopped and looked down. In the surface of the water he saw his own reflection shining up at him.

The dog did not realise he was looking at himself. He thought that he was looking at another dog with a piece of meat in its mouth.

'Hello, that piece of meat is bigger than mine,' he thought. 'I'll grab it and run.'

At that he dropped his own piece of meat in order to snatch the piece the other dog had. Of course his piece of meat fell into the stream and sank to the bottom, leaving the dog with nothing.

| Moral | Be content with what you have. |

# THE CROW AND THE WATER JUG

The sun had been shining for days, making everything dry and hot. A crow flew on and on with feeble wings, looking in vain for something to drink. She knew that if she did not find water soon she would die of thirst.

Weakly she fluttered to the ground, almost giving up hope. An object standing on its own on a heap of pebbles caught her eye. Slowly the bird hopped over to it. The object was an old water jug.

Without much hope the crow peered into the jug. A croak of surprise. escaped her lips. There was water in the bottom of the jug!

Eagerly the crow tried to push her head down to the water. Her beak was too short to reach it. She knew that if she pushed the jug over, the water would just run away and soak into the ground.

Then the crow had an idea. In her beak she started picking up the pebbles lying around, and one by one, dropping them into the bottom of the jug. As the heap of pebbles inside the jug grew, so the level of the water rose, until the crow was able to drink.

| **Moral** | *Necessity is the mother of invention.* |

14

# THE WOLF AND THE GOAT

A cunning wolf saw a goat nibbling grass at the top of a hill.

"What a good dinner you would make," said the wolf to himself, licking his lips hungrily.

He walked forward and gazed longingly up at the goat. He was not nearly as sure-footed as the other animal. There was no way in which he could climb the cliff and fall upon the goat. Somehow he had to persuade the goat to come down to him.

"Good morning, Madam Goat," he called out, putting on his most engaging smile. "Please be careful. It is so dangerously high on that cliff. I should hate you to come to any harm. I'll tell you what! Why don't you come down here, where the grass is fresh and green. I speak to you as a friend."

The goat was not to be fooled. She looked down at the wolf and shook her head.

"You can't trick me," she called down. "You don't care whether the grass I eat is fresh and green, or dry and brown. All that you want to do is to eat me!"

| Moral | *Look before you leap.* |

# THE OXEN AND THE WAGON

Two oxen were pulling a loaded wagon along a road. It was very hard work. The road was full of holes. The wagon was heavy and hard to pull. The oxen had to strain every muscle to make the wagon move at all.

Behind them the wagon was making a great fuss, complaining all the time. Its wheels groaned and creaked.

Suddenly, one of the oxen could no longer bear the dreadful noise being made by the wagon. He looked back over his aching shoulder and said, "What have you got to complain about? My brother and I are doing all the work!"

| Moral | *They complain most who suffer least.* |

# HERCULES AND THE WAGONER

A man was driving his horse and wagon along a muddy lane when the wheels of his cart sank deep into the mud. The man got down and tried to push the wagon along. It was no use. The wagon was stuck.

The man lifted his head and cried in despair. "Everything happens to me!" he wailed. "Why doesn't someone come and help me? What about the mighty Hercules? He is the strongest man on earth. Where is he now that I need him?"

Hercules heard his name being called and came to see what was wanted of him.

"Stop moaning and put your shoulder to the wheel," he told the wagoner sternly. "How can you expect others to help you, if you do not help yourself? If you show that you are willing to do your share, I will gladly help you."

| Moral | *Heaven helps those who help themselves.* |

# THE MOON AND HER MOTHER

The moon was so beautiful that she became vain and wanted to look even lovelier. She asked her mother to make her a gown that she could wear as she drifted lazily across the sky. To her surprise her mother shook her head sadly.

"Alas, that is something I can never do for you," she said.

"But why not?" cried the moon, greatly disappointed. At that moment, she wanted a gown more than anything else in the whole world.

"Think for a while," advised her mother, "and then you will see that I could never make a gown that would fit you."

"But why not?" the moon sobbed.

"Because you are always changing," her mother told her. "At times you are so thin you can slide under a closed door. Yet at other times you are so full and round, people could easily take you for a cheese. And between these two sizes, you are neither fat nor thin but all different shapes."

| Moral | *Someone who is always changing cannot expect others to regard him as one particular thing.* |
|---|---|

# THE GREEDY FOX

It was the custom of a group of shepherds to hide their dinners in the shelter of a hollow tree before setting out to look after their sheep.

A clever fox saw what they did. For a number of days he hid, and watched the shepherds until he was sure that they did not come back to the tree for their food for some hours each day.

One morning, he watched the men hide their food as usual and then leave. The fox waited until the shepherds were out of sight and then he ran over to the hollow tree. The gap in the trunk was narrow, but by pulling in his sides he managed to squeeze inside.

Once he was in the tree, the hungry fox began eating the food. He ate and he ate until he could eat no more.

Then the fox tried to squeeze himself out of the tree again. To his horror he found that he could not do so. He had eaten so much that his stomach had grown plump. No matter how hard he tried he could not squeeze in his sides enough to get through the gap in the tree.

The trapped fox set up such a great howling that one of his friends heard him and came running over to the tree.

"Help me!" sobbed the fox from inside the tree. "I have eaten so much that I have grown too fat to get out of this hole."

"There is only one thing you can do," said his friend, shaking his head.

"What's that?" demanded the fox, hopefully.

"You will have to wait there until you grow thin enough to get out again," his friend told him bluntly.

| Moral | *We should think before we act.* |

22

# THE DONKEY AND HIS SHADOW

A traveller hired a donkey to take him to the next town. He agreed a fee with the owner of the donkey.

"There is just one drawback," explained the donkey's owner. "My donkey won't walk very far unless I hit him with a stick now and again. You ride on his back, and I'll walk along behind you with a stick, until we reach the town."

It was a very hot day, but the two men made good progress, with the traveller riding on the donkey and the owner walking behind with a stick to prod the donkey. In the middle of the day, with the sun at its hottest, they stopped for a rest.

"I shall sit in the shade of the donkey," said the traveller, dismounting.

"Oh no you won't," snapped the donkey's owner. "That's where I'm going to rest. It's the only shade for miles around."

"I've hired the donkey, so I should sit in its shade," argued the traveller.

"Not at all," shouted the owner. "You only hired the donkey, you did not hire its shadow. That belongs to me."

The owner was so angry that he gave the traveller a push. The traveller pushed back. The owner hit the traveller. The traveller hit the owner back. In a moment, the two men were standing toe to toe, fighting furiously.

While the two men fought over his shadow, the donkey grew bored and trotted off over the hill. Soon he was out of sight, taking his shadow with him.

| Moral | *Most arguments are useless.* |

# THE BOY AND THE WOLF

A wolf was prowling over the fields looking for food. A boy saw the wolf coming and turned to flee. He realised that the wolf would catch up with him in a few seconds, so instead he tried to hide in some long grass.

The wolf found the boy's hiding place almost at once. He came loping over to the child, his teeth bared.

"Please, Mr Wolf, do not eat me," begged the boy, trembling with fear.

The wolf hesitated. He had intended to kill and eat the boy, but he had to admit that he had already caught plenty of small animals that day, and he was not really very hungry. He decided instead to have some sport with the terrified child.

"Very well," he said, licking his lips. "I will spare your life, if you tell me three things which are so true that I cannot possibly disagree with them."

The boy thought rapidly, knowing that his life depended upon his three answers.

"Well," he said slowly, "it's a pity that you saw me."

"That's true," agreed the wolf. "That's one answer."

"And," went on the boy, gaining confidence, "it's a pity I let you see me."

"That's true as well," nodded the wolf. "Very well, you have two out of three. Everything depends upon your third answer."

"Thirdly," said the boy in a rush, "people hate wolves because they attack sheep for no reason at all."

The wolf was silent for a long time. The boy wondered if he had been too bold. But this wolf was fair-minded.

"I suppose that is true from your point of view," he admitted. "Very well, you may go."

| Moral | *A fair-minded person tries to see both sides of an argument.* |
|-------|----------------------------------------------------------------|

27

# THE FOX AND THE BRAMBLE

The fox was tired and hungry. He had been prowling over the fields all day, looking for food. Now he was on his way home and he was in no mood to be delayed.

He came to a hedge which stood between him and his lair. He ought to walk along the side of the hedge until he found a hole, but he was too tired and fed-up to bother. He decided to push his way through the hedge, to save time.

The fox leapt across the ditch towards the hedge. As he did so, his foot slipped. Desperately the fox thrust out his paws and caught hold of a bramble to stop himself falling. The bramble scratched the fox badly.

"I would have been better off letting myself fall, than ask you for help," he complained sourly.

"You should have had more sense than to clutch a bramble," said the hedge.

| Moral | *We should use our judgement before coming to a decision.* |

# THE FOX AND THE GRAPES

The fox came padding across the fields in the golden sunlight. His pointed ears were alert. He sniffed the air for any sign of danger. He was a fox and all men were against him.

At the edge of a vineyard he stopped. Thousands of tangled vines crept over high, wooden frames. Hanging from the vines were great bunches of juicy grapes.

"I'll steal some before the owner comes," the fox decided.

He reached up and snapped at the nearest grapes. The bunch was too high. Snarling with rage he backed off and leapt into the air, snapping with his great jaws.

He missed! Howling with rage, the fox tried again. For over an hour he ran and jumped, ran and jumped. He could not reach any of the grapes.

At last he gave up and slunk away. "I didn't want those grapes at all, really," he muttered. "They were sour and useless!"

| Moral | *Sometimes when we cannot get what we want, we pretend that we did not want it anyway.* |

# THE WILD BOAR AND THE FOX

A fox was trotting through the forest. He noticed how peaceful everything seemed. He could hear no sounds of wild animals fighting each other, and there were no signs of any hunters in search of prey.

'How nice this is,' thought the fox as he went on his way.

After a while he came across a wild boar. The animal was busily sharpening its tusks on a tree, rubbing them against the bark. The fox stopped to watch.

"You silly animal," he yawned. "Why are you wasting your time doing that? There is no need for it. It is a very quiet day here in the forest. There are no hunters about to fear."

"You may be right," grunted the boar, not stopping. "But that isn't the point. When my life is in danger, I must be ready to defend myself at once. I won't have time to stop and sharpen my tusks first!"

| Moral | *Be prepared.* |

# THE HOUND AND THE HARE

A hare was playing happily on her own in a field when suddenly a hound came bounding up to her. The hare squealed with terror, thinking that the hound would kill her. The great dog snapped at her with fierce teeth. The hare closed her eyes, expecting the worst. To her surprise, the dog did not bite her. Instead he stopped snarling and snapping. The hare opened her eyes and peered at the hound.

"Come and play with me," invited the dog, wagging his tail.

"Certainly not," snapped the hare. "I wouldn't dream of it."

"Why not?" asked the disappointed hound.

"Because I don't know what to make of you," replied the hare. "If you are my friend why do you try to bite me, and if you are my enemy why do you want to play with me?"

**Moral**    *We like people to show themselves to us as they really are.*

# THE GNAT AND THE BULL

The gnat was a small insect but it had a great idea of its own importance. One fine day it grew tired of flying and landed on the horn of a great bull grazing in a field. The animal went on chewing, taking no notice of the small gnat. The insect rested in the sun until it felt ready to carry on flying. Before it left, it looked down politely at the bull.

"I'm afraid I must be on my way now," it said. "Thank you for allowing me to rest on your horn. I would like to stay and chat, but I should be on my way."

"I couldn't care less what you do," grunted the bull. "I did not notice you come, and I shall not notice when you go."

| Moral | *We often seem more important to ourselves than we do to others.* |

# THE PIG AND THE SHEEP

A pig managed to escape from its sty. It ran away and joined a flock of sheep grazing in a field. The sheep made friends with the pig and allowed it to stay with them.

Then the farmer came along. When he saw the pig he picked it up and carried it off under his arm.

"I'll take you to the butcher," he told the animal.

At this the pig set up a dreadful squealing and wriggling as it tried to escape. The grazing sheep were amazed.

"What are you making such a fuss about?" one of them asked. "We don't make a fuss like that when the farmer carries us off."

"Perhaps you don't," squealed the pig. "He wants a lot more from me than he does from you. He wants you for your wool, but he wants me for my bacon!"

| Moral | *We should not make up our minds until we know the truth.* |

# THE TOWN MOUSE AND THE COUNTRY MOUSE

The Country Mouse watched sadly as his friend the Town Mouse packed his bags to leave. The Town Mouse had just spent a few unhappy days at the Country Mouse's home under a hedge in a field.

"You poor thing," said the Town Mouse with pity in his voice. "You live so poorly in the country, with only roots and corn to eat. Come back with me to the town and I will show you what good living is like."

The two tiny creatures made the long journey to the house where the Town Mouse lived, in the great city. At first, the Country Mouse thought that life in the town was indeed wonderful. He had never seen such food as there was in the larder. He had just started to nibble some of the dates and figs stored there, when the door opened.

"Quick!" squealed the Town Mouse in a panic. "We must hide in my hole!"

In an instant the Country Mouse found himself squashed against his friend in a small, dark hole. It was hot and very crowded.

After quite a long time, the Town Mouse said that it would be safe to leave the hole. The two animals came out into the larder, trying to stretch their cramped legs and shake the kinks from their tails. Still shaking with fright the Country Mouse picked up a fig again. Before he could eat it the door swung open again.

"Quick! Hide!" squealed the Town Mouse.

Yet again the Country Mouse found himself pressed against his friend in the tiny hole, with hardly room to twitch his whiskers, and with his heart beating wildly.

"That's it!" he told his friend firmly. "You may have very good food here, but what's the point of having good food if you are always too frightened to eat it? I'm going back home."

So the Country Mouse packed his little bag and scurried back along the city streets until he reached his beloved fields again. With great contentment he crept back into his little hole under the hedge.

"This is the place for me," he said to himself, looking round at all the things he loved so much. "I like being able to twitch my whiskers and flick my tail whenever I want to. The Town Mouse can keep his old town!"

| Moral | *Our own home always seems the best to us.* |

# THE HARE AND THE TORTOISE

The hare was a very fast runner, like most of his kind and he was always teasing the tortoise.

"You are so very slow," he would sigh as the tortoise ambled by. "I wouldn't be surprised if you were the slowest creature in the world. I don't suppose you even know how to hurry."

"Oh, I think I could move fast enough if I had to," said the tortoise happily, inching his way along.

The hare laughed. "What a funny idea," he jeered. "Why, I suppose you even think you could beat me in a race."

The tortoise stopped and thought. "Yes, I do," he said finally.

"Very well," the hare told him indignantly. "If you want to make a fool of yourself, we'll have a race."

The proposed contest aroused a great deal of interest among all the animals. On the day of the race they turned out in great numbers to see the fox start the two creatures off over the course he had arranged.

The hare set off at such a great pace, he soon left the tortoise far behind and out of sight. Before long the winning post was looming up before the running hare. Suddenly an idea came to the animal and he skidded to a halt.

"I'll really rub it in," he said to himself. "I'll wait here until the poor tortoise comes into sight and then he can see me skip past the winning post."

With that idea in mind, the hare sat down under a tree and waited for the tortoise to appear. It was a very hot day and before long the hare had fallen fast asleep.

Meanwhile, the slow old tortoise had been plodding on doggedly. He passed the tree and the sleeping hare. Then he passed the winning post. The cheers of the watching animals woke the hare. To his amazement he saw that he had lost the race.

| Moral | *Slow and steady can win the race.* |

# THE BIRDS, THE BEASTS AND THE BAT

The birds and beasts were at war. Their battles were fierce and frequent. Sometimes the birds won, swooping down out of the sun and attacking the animals. Sometimes the beasts won, creeping up on the birds as they searched for food on the ground, and leaping on them.

But there was one creature who was always on the winning side. He never lost, because he kept on changing sides. He would fight for the birds until they looked like losing, and then change sides. For a time he would fight for the animals, and then if the birds gained the upper hand, he would change back and join *them*.

This creature was the bat. He thought he was a very clever fellow, always being on the winning side.

In the end the war ended. The birds and the beasts agreed to live in peace for ever.

"Now I shall get my reward," the bat told himself. "Everyone will think I'm a fine fellow. After all, *I* was never on the losing side. I helped both sides. In fact, the birds and the beasts may make me their king!"

It did not work out like that at all. Neither the birds nor the beasts would have anything to do with him!

"You are a traitor!" they told the amazed bat. "You are loyal to no one. You only serve yourself. You let down both sides in the war. We want nothing more to do with you."

From that day to this the bat was an outcast, ignored by both the birds and the beasts.

| Moral | *People are expected to be loyal and to stick by their friends.* |

# THE TRAVELLERS AND THE PLANE TREE

It was a hot and dusty afternoon. Two travellers came into sight. They were very tired. They had been walking since early morning. All that time the sun had been beating down on them. There had been no sign of any kind of shade.

Suddenly, in the distance, the travellers saw a solitary plane tree. Their hearts leapt with joy.

"Shelter at last!" cried one of the men.

Both men forced themselves to hurry forwards towards the distant tree. They reached it and stood beneath its leafy branches. Then they sank gratefully to the ground, relaxing in the shade, glad to escape at last from the blazing heat of the sun.

After a time, as both men lay on their backs looking up into the branches of the tree, one of the travellers spoke.

"It's funny," he remarked.

"What is?" asked his companion.

"This plane tree we're resting under," said the traveller. "Have you ever stopped to think how useless it is? It bears no fruit. It is of no use to man at all."

Although it said nothing to them, the plane tree overheard the two travellers' discussion.

'What ungrateful people,' it thought bitterly. 'They take shelter from the sun beneath my branches, and are glad to do so. But do they thank me for it? They do not! Instead, at this very moment they are enjoying the coolness and shade I am providing for them and they lie there and complain that I am useless!'

| **Moral** | *We are not always grateful for help when it is offered.* |

# THE ASTRONOMER

An absent-minded astronomer was interested in nothing but the stars. Every night he would go out and study them in the sky.

One evening he was walking along as usual, his head in the air and his eyes fixed on the stars. He did not notice that there was a deep well in front of him. As he made his way along, he suddenly tripped and fell into the well.

"Help!" he shouted. "Help me someone!"

He sat at the bottom of the well, soaked to the skin and calling for help. A passer-by heard his shouts and peered down the hole at him.

"Please help me," begged the astronomer. "I was so busy looking at the stars, I did not notice this hole."

"That's your fault," the passer-by told him. "You should have looked where you were going."

| Moral | *It is no use fixing our minds on higher things if we ignore what is going on around us.* |

# THE HORSE AND HIS RIDER

It was a fine spring day when a rich young man went out for a ride in the country on his new horse. Unfortunately, although he did not know it, his horse was still almost wild. As soon as it felt its rider in the saddle, the horse's ears went back and it bolted wildly along the quiet lane.

In vain, the young rider tried to control his mount. It was no use. All that he could do was to throw his arms about the neck of the animal and cling on as best he could.

"Where are you going in such a hurry?" shouted the young man's friend, leaping for the safety of a ditch.

"How should I know?" shouted the young man as he was carried away. "I'm not in charge any more. You had better ask the horse!"

| Moral | *We should all make sure that we know who is in charge.* |

# THE BALD HUNTSMAN

A man who had lost all his hair bought himself a wig made out of real human hair. Then he went out hunting with his friends.

As the huntsman was riding over a field, a gust of wind blew his top-hat from his head. His new wig went spinning off with his hat, leaving him quite bald again.

The other huntsmen thought that their friend would be very angry at what had happened. When they rode up to him, however, they saw that he was roaring with laughter until the tears ran down his face.

"What's so funny about losing your wig?" asked one.

"I was just thinking," chuckled the jolly huntsman. "If the hair that wig was made from could not stick to the head it belonged to, how could I expect it to stick to mine?"

| Moral | *Laugh and the world laughs with you.* |

# THE HUNTER AND THE WOODMAN

A hunter armed with a rifle, walked bravely through the forest, saying loudly that he was looking for a lion to shoot. Secretly, he was not quite as brave as he would like people to think he was.

After a long walk he came across a woodman cutting a tree. The hunter stopped.

"Hey there," he called. "I'm looking for the tracks of a lion. Can you tell me where I might find some?"

The woodman put down his axe and nodded.

"Yes, certainly," he said. "Come with me and I will show you the lion himself."

At this the hunter turned pale and his knees shook.

"N . . . n . . . no thank you," he said, turning and hurrying away. "I . . . I'm not looking for the l . . . l . . . lion himself, only his tracks."

| **Moral** | *People are not always as brave as they say they are.* |

# THE FOX AND THE CROW

A fox was prowling along looking in vain for food. It had been a long day and he was very hungry.

"What I would like more than anything else in the world," he said longingly to himself, "is a nice piece of cheese."

Just as the thought passed through his head, the fox glanced up at the branches of a tree he was passing. To his amazement he saw a black crow sitting in the tree. In her beak was a piece of cheese. The fox licked his lips greedily. Somehow or other he had to get that cheese from the bird.

"Oh, Crow," he said admiringly, as if butter would not melt in his mouth. "What a beautiful bird you are. Your feathers are so soft and black, your beak so beautifully curved. If only . . ."

The fox stopped and shook his head doubtfully. The crow looked down, wondering what the fox was going to say next.

"If only," went on the fox, "your voice was as beautiful as your appearance, you would be a queen among birds."

Greatly flattered, the bird opened her beak and cawed loudly to show that she could sing. As she did so, the piece of cheese fell to the ground. The fox picked the cheese up and ran off with it.

| Moral | *Beware of flattery, it may not be meant.* |

# THE BEE-KEEPER AND THE BEES

There was once a bee-keeper who looked after a number of bee-hives. The bee-keeper kept his bees for their honey and like all good bee-keepers he never took all the honey from the hives, but always left some for the bees.

One day a thief waited until the bee-keeper had gone off for his lunch and all the bees were out of the hives looking for pollen, from which they make their honey.

The thief was very greedy. He broke up the hives and took every scrap of honey that he could find. Then he ran off with it.

When the bee-keeper came back and saw what had happened, he was very upset.

"My poor bees!" he cried. "What will they do when they see their hives broken and all their honey stolen? I must try to put things right before they get back."

He set out to do this. He was just picking up the pieces of one of the broken hives when a swarm of bees returned. They saw all the damage and the broken honeycombs which had once held their honey. They also saw the bee-keeper standing over their ruined home. They thought that he must have destroyed it.

BZZZZZZZZ! The bees were very angry. They attacked the poor bee-keeper and stung him again and again.

"It's not fair!" he shouted. "You let the man who stole your honey go free but you sting your friend and helper!"

| Moral | *Things are not always what they seem.* |

# THE BOY AND THE HAZELNUTS

A greedy boy saw a jar of hazelnuts standing on a table. He licked his lips and stole up to the jar. Plunging his hand inside, he grabbed the biggest handful he could take.

"Hazelnuts!" he crowed gleefully. "How I love them!"

But the boy had picked up so many nuts that he could not pull his hand out of the jar. He roared with rage. Then he wept in despair. If he let the nuts go, he would be able to take his hand out of the jar. But he wanted those nuts so badly!

An onlooker helped him with some good advice.

"Don't be so greedy," said the man. "Take half the amount of hazelnuts and your hand will come out of the jar easily."

| Moral | *Do not attempt too much at one time.* |

# THE TWO POTS

The river was in flood, sweeping everything along with it. On top of the water, bobbing helplessly along, were two pots. One of the pots was made from the strong mixture of metals known as brass. The other pot was just as beautiful but it was not nearly as strong, because it was made out of clay.

"Come over here and stay close to me," the brass pot invited the clay pot. "I will look after you. I am very strong. Nothing can break me. I might dent a little, but that is all. As for you, poor thing, I know how weak clay pots are. You are so easily broken. Come here, I say, and let me guard you."

"No, thank you," called out the clay pot, keeping as far away from the brass pot as it possibly could.

"Why not?" asked the brass pot, rather hurt. "Why don't you float down the river with me?"

"Well, I know you mean your offer kindly," said the clay pot, drifting away quickly, "but you are so much stronger than I am. One tiny knock from you and I would break into a thousand pieces."

| Moral | *Equals make the best friends.* |

56

# THE LARK AND THE FARMER

When it was time to build her nest, the lark decided to make her home in a cornfield and not in a tree like most other birds. She laid her eggs in this nest and watched them hatch out into young birds. Life was very good among the waving corn.

Then one day, the farmer who owned the field came walking across to look at it.

"Hmm, very nice," he said. "This corn is just about ready to harvest. I think I'll have a word with my neighbours and ask them to help me gather it in."

At this the young larks were very frightened and set up a great twittering.

"Quick, mother, we must move before our nest is destroyed!"

Their mother was too wise to be worried by such talk.

"Hush, my darlings," she soothed. "There is nothing to worry about yet. A man who talks about going to his neighbours for help can be in no great hurry. We can wait a little longer."

A few days later, when the corn was so ripe it was falling to the ground, the farmer walked across the field again.

"I must hire some men and gather in this corn at once," he said.

"Come, my children," sighed the mother lark. "Now the farmer is relying upon himself, not others. It is time for us to move."

| Moral | *If we really want something done, it is best to do it ourselves.* |

# THE CAGED BIRD AND THE BAT

Once there was a bird which lived in a wood. The bird sang all day long and his song rang throughout the wood.

A bird-catcher decided to trap this bird with a net and sell it for a great deal of money. The bird flew into the net and was caught.

The bird-catcher sold the bird to a man who lived in a cottage. The man put the singing bird in a cage, just outside the cottage window. To his surprise the bird would not sing at all during the day. It would only sing at night when most other birds were asleep.

The wild creatures which lived nearby wondered why this was so. They asked a bat to go and find out. The bat slept by day, hanging upside-down in a barn, but flew about at night when the caged bird was singing.

The bat flew to the bird's cage and asked the bird, "Why do you sing at night instead of during the day?"

"The bird-catcher caught me because I guided him to me with my song in the day-time," explained the bird sadly. "Because I sang by day I lost my freedom. Now I only sing during the dark hours."

"It's a bit late for that," the bat told the bird. "If you had only thought of that when you were free, you would not have been caught."

| **Moral** | *It pays to think before we act.* |

# A BOY BATHING

A boy thought that it would be fun to go for a swim in a river. His friends warned him that it was very deep, but he would not listen to them.

Soon after he had dived in, he found that the water was far too deep. He grew very frightened.

"Help me!" he cried. "I am drowning!"

A man happened to be walking by with his dog, along the bank of the river. He looked angrily at the poor boy.

"You silly lad!" he shouted. "Don't you know how dangerous that river is? You are a young fool!"

"Please sir," wailed the boy, feeling himself sinking, "if it's all the same to you, could you save me first and tell me off later?"

| Moral | *We need to be helped, not scolded, when we are in trouble.* |
| --- | --- |

# THE FOX AND THE STORK

A fox decided to play a joke upon a stork. In order to do this he invited the bird to dinner in his den. When the stork arrived, the fox served a delicious soup in a flat dish.

"Mm, this soup tastes good," said the fox, lapping greedily from the flat dish, his nose only a few inches from it. "What do you think of it, my friend?"

"How can I tell?" grumbled the stork, pecking vainly at the flat dish with her long beak. "This dish is too flat. I cannot get any soup into my mouth."

This was just what the sly old fox had hoped would happen. He had upset the stork and made her look silly. He thought this was very funny and finished the soup himself with a sly smile upon his face. The stork made one or two more efforts to peck at the soup, but then gave up and went home, deciding to get her own back on the fox.

A few days later the stork had made her plans. She invited the fox to come and have dinner with her in her home by the water's edge. She too prepared soup for the meal. She served it in a jug which was wide at the bottom and narrow at the top.

"Let us begin," said the stork, dipping her head into the jug and taking a long sip. "Mm, this is good! What do you think of it, my friend?"

"How can I tell?" grumbled the fox, trying in vain to get his head into the mouth of the jug. "I cannot reach the soup to lap it up!"

"What a shame," said the stork calmly.

She said nothing else, but finished the soup herself, while the fox looked on, angrily.

In the end, the fox went home in a bad mood. The tables had been turned on him, but for some reason he did not think it was funny.

| **Moral** | *Something which seems funny when it happens to someone else, may not seem so funny when it happens to us.* |

# THE BOASTING TRAVELLER

A traveller was boasting about the wonderful places he had been to and the clever things he had done. The people listening to him had grown bored of his constant boasting.

"Once," said the traveller loudly, "when I was in Rhodes, I entered a jumping competition. As a matter of fact, I jumped twice as far as anyone has ever jumped before. If you don't believe me, go to Rhodes and ask someone there."

"If you can really jump that far," said one of his audience, who had not believed one word the traveller had said, " . . . there is no need to go to Rhodes to prove it. You could do something else."

"What do you mean?" asked the puzzled traveller.

"Well," said the man, "you can jump here and prove it to us now."

| Moral | *Deeds speak louder than words.* |

# THE MICE IN COUNCIL

A cat was chasing all the mice and killing those she caught. The mice called a great meeting to try to think of some way of making themselves safe from the cat.

The meeting lasted a long time. Many ideas were put forward by the mice at the council, but none of them seemed any good. Finally, one bright young mouse stepped forward.

"I've got it!" he said excitedly. "The reason why the cat catches so many of us is that we don't hear her coming. Is that right?"

"Of course it is," said another mouse. "That doesn't help us much."

"I haven't finished yet," the first mouse told him impatiently. "What we need is something to warn us of the cat's approach. Well, I know what to do. We must tie a bell round the cat's neck. That way, every time the cat comes near us, we will hear the bell tinkling and have time to hide."

"What a good idea!" squeaked the other mice. "Well done! You have solved all our problems. All we have to do is find a bell and tie it round the cat's neck."

The other mice started to cheer and squeal excitedly, but then an old and very wise mouse who had taken no part in the meeting so far spoke up from a corner.

"Just a minute," he said. "It may be a good idea, but tell me this. Is anyone here willing to risk his life by going up to the cat and putting the bell round her neck?"

No one answered. In a moment all the mice had left the meeting and the room was empty. No one was prepared to put the bell on the cat.

| Moral | *It is no use having bright ideas unless we are willing to put them into practice.* |
|---|---|

# THE LION AND THE MOUSE

The lion was proud and strong, and king of the jungle. One day while he was sleeping, a tiny mouse ran over his face. The great lion awoke with a roar. He caught the mouse with one mighty paw and raised the other to squash the tiny creature which had annoyed him.

"Oh, please, mighty lion," squeaked the mouse. "Please do not kill me. Let me go, I beg you. If you do, one day I may be able to help you in some way."

This greatly amused the lion. The thought that such a small and frightened creature as a mouse might be able to help the king of the jungle was so funny that he did not have the heart to kill the mouse.

"Go away," he growled, "before I change my mind."

A few days later, a party of hunters came into the jungle. They decided to

try to capture the lion. They climbed two trees, one on either side of the path, and held a net over the path.

Later in the day the lion came loping along. At once the hunters dropped their net on the great beast. The lion roared and struggled, but he could not escape.

The hunters went off to eat, leaving the lion trapped in the net, unable to move. The lion roared for help, but the only creature in the jungle who dared come near was the tiny mouse.

"Oh, it's you," groaned the lion. "There's nothing you can do to help me. You're too small."

"I may be small," said the mouse, "but I have sharp teeth and I owe you a good turn."

Then the mouse began to nibble at the net. Before long he had made a hole big enough to allow the lion to crawl through and make his escape into the jungle.

| Moral | *Sometimes the weak are able to help the strong.* |

# THE PEACOCK AND THE CRANE

Once there was a peacock who was very proud and vain. He boasted to everyone about his beautiful feathers. If it rained, he would stand looking at his reflection in puddles.

"Just look at my tail!" he would crow. "Look at the colours of my feathers. I am so beautiful! I must be the most beautiful bird in the world!"

At this he would open his tail like a great fan and stand waiting for someone to come along and admire him.

The other birds became annoyed at the boasts of the proud peacock and tried to think of a way of taking him down a peg or two. It was the great bird called the crane who had an idea.

"Leave it to me," he told the others. "I'll make that vain peacock look foolish."

One morning the crane strolled past the peacock. As usual the peacock was preening his feathers.

"Look how beautiful I am!" he cried. "You are so plain and dull, Crane. Why don't you try to look a little smarter?"

"Your feathers may be more beautiful than mine," said the crane calmly. "But I notice that you cannot fly. Your beautiful feathers are not strong enough to lift you from the ground. I may be dull, but my wings can carry me into the sky!"

| Moral | *We may lose in one way, but gain in another.* |

# THE CRAB AND HIS MOTHER

A crab lived with his mother at the bottom of the sea. The mother crab was very proud of her son, but she was always nagging him to do better.

One morning she noticed her son scuttling across the sea-bed in the sideways motion that crabs have. "I wish you would walk forwards," she grumbled. "It would look much nicer."

"I will, Mother, if you will show me how," replied her son.

The crab tried, but found that she could only walk sideways.

| Moral | *We should not criticise people for what is not their fault.* |
|---|---|

# JUPITER AND THE TORTOISE

Thousands of years ago, the tortoise did not carry his shell on his back. Then something happened which saw to it that for ever more the tortoise and his shell were always together.

It started when the great god Jupiter, invited all the animals to a great feast. Every animal that lived came to this feast, except for the tortoise.

Jupiter was so disappointed. He had hoped that every creature under the sun would come to his feast, but the tortoise had spoiled that.

"Perhaps he is ill," worried the god. "I had better go and see."

So Jupiter made his way to the home of the tortoise. When he arrived he found the creature looking perfectly well.

"Why didn't you come to my feast?" asked the god.

"I didn't feel like it," yawned the tortoise. "I wanted to stay at home instead."

"Indeed?" said the god angrily. "In that case, for the rest of time wherever you go, you had better carry your home with you."

And that is just what happened, from that day to this.

| Moral | *We had better be careful what we say in case people take us at our word.* |

76

# THE GRASSHOPPER AND THE ANTS

All through the long summer days, the ants had worked hard gathering food for the winter days when snow lay deep on the ground.

As they gathered their food and put it in their store-house the idle grasshopper looked at them and laughed.

"You fools!" he called. "Why do you work when the sun is high in the sky? This is a time for singing and playing."

The ants paid no attention to him. They went on working hard, collecting enough food to see them through the long winter days and nights. As they did so the grasshopper lay in the sun, singing happily.

But soon summer was over. Winter ruled the land, covering everything with snow and ice. There was no food to be found anywhere. The grasshopper, who had stored no food in the summer months, was starving. He limped along to the store-house where the ants had stored their food.

"What do you want?" asked the ants, as they carried on sweeping, tidying and sorting. The ants were always busy.

"I am very hungry," begged the grasshopper. "Please give me some of the food you have saved, or I will starve to death."

"You should have thought of that in the summer when you were busy with your playing and singing," said the ants. "If you spent the summer singing, then maybe you should spend the winter dancing, and not bother about eating at all."

The ants would not give the grasshopper a single scrap of their food, and he went away sad and hungry.

| Moral | *We should always make plans for the future.* |  |

# THE MAN AND THE SATYR

There was once a man who shared a house with a satyr. A satyr is a wood-god, half goat and half human. For some time they lived together happily. Then one winter it became very cold. The man started blowing on his frozen hands.

"Why are you doing that?" asked the satyr.

"To warm them, of course," said the man. "I always blow on my hands to warm them if they are cold."

That same evening they had porridge for supper. The porridge was very hot. The man was afraid that it would burn his tongue. He lifted the bowl to his lips and blew on it. The satyr watched in amazement.

"Now what are you doing?" he asked.

"Blowing on my porridge, of course," said the man.

"But why?" demanded the satyr.

"To cool it, you silly satyr," the man said in surprise.

The satyr shook his head and stood up.

"That does it," he said. "I'm off."

"What do you mean?" the man asked. "Where are you going?"

"As far away from you as I can get," replied the satyr. "I'm not going to stay with someone who can blow hot and cold with the same breath."

| Moral | *People like us to remain constant and do the same things all the time*. |

# THE FISHERMAN AND THE SPRAT

It had been a bad day for the poor fisherman. He had sailed his small craft out into the wide sea at dawn. All day he had been casting his nets into the water and then drawing them out again. Each time he did so, the nets remained empty.

"Can there be a single fish left in the sea, I wonder?" the man grumbled. "It certainly doesn't seem so."

He was about to give up and sail sadly back to port, when he drew in his nets for the last time. Something was wriggling in the bottom of one of the nets. His heart leaping, the fisherman hurried forward to see what he had caught. To his disgust he saw that he had caught one small sprat, the tiniest of fish.

This particular sprat was so small that it fitted easily into the palm of the fisherman's hand.

"Please let me go," begged the small fish. "You can see for yourself that I am no use to you as I am. But if you throw me back into the water, I shall grow up into a fine big fish. Then you can catch me again in a year's time, when I will make a meal."

"No way," said the man. "If I let you go you would vanish!"

| **Moral** | *A fish in the hand is worth two in the sea.* |

# THE STAG AT THE POOL

A fine stag went to the pool to drink. When he had drank enough, he stood and gazed at his own reflection. His great twisted horns called antlers looked magnificent.

"I really do have a very fine pair of antlers," the stag said proudly. "They are very handsome indeed."

He turned away. As he did so he caught a glimpse of his legs reflected in the pool. Some of his feeling of pride left him.

"What a pity my legs are not as fine as my antlers," he said sadly. "It is very true that my legs are far too weak and thin. I wish I could do something to improve them."

A lion who had been creeping up on the stag suddenly leapt out at him. At once the stag fled. The ground ahead was open and free from trees. The stag's legs served him well. Soon he drew ahead of the lion and dashed into a forest. Unfortunately his fine antlers became tangled in the branches of a tree, forcing the stag to come to a halt until the lion caught up with him.

"What a fool I was!" cried the stag as the lion leapt upon him. "The legs I despised have served me well, while the antlers of which I was so proud have let me down."

| Moral | *What is worth most is often valued least.* |

# MERCURY AND THE WOODMAN

An honest woodman lived with his family in a forest. He worked very hard all day, cutting down trees with his trusted axe. One day he was walking by the side of a deep, fast-flowing river, carrying his axe in his hand. He slipped and the axe fell from his hand into the river.

"Help!" cried the woodman. "The water is too deep and I cannot get my axe back. Without it I cannot work. I shall starve!"

Mercury, one of the ancient gods, heard the woodman's lament. He came down to earth and dived into the deep river, coming up with an axe made of pure gold.

"That is not mine," said the honest woodman, and he would not take the axe from the god.

Again Mercury dived to the bottom of the river. This time he returned with an axe made of pure silver. The honest woodman shook his head.

"That is not my axe, either," he said. "I cannot take what does not belong to me."

For a third time Mercury dived to the bed of the river. When he came out again he was carrying the woodman's battered old axe.

"That's my axe!" cried the woodman, and he took it eagerly.

Mercury was so impressed by the honesty of the woodman that he gave him both the silver and the gold axes as a reward. The man took the three axes back to his family.

Another woodman heard what had happened. He went to the same part of the river and dropped his axe into the water. Then he made a great fuss.

"Oh, Mercury, please help me!" he cried.

The god came down and dived into the river, returning with an axe made of gold.

"That's mine!" lied the woodman and he took the golden axe.

Mercury punished the man by making the golden axe vanish. The woodman's own axe was left lying at the bottom of the river, where all could see it, but no one could reach it.

| **Moral** | *Honesty is the best policy.* |

# THE WOLF AND THE HORSE

A wolf was slinking across the fields, looking for mischief. He passed by a field of oats, waving in the soft breeze. The wolf stopped hopefully, sniffing around for the scent of some small creature he could hunt down and eat. There was no sign of any living thing, however, so the disappointed wolf went on his way across the fields.

Some time later, the wolf met a horse. The hair on the wolf's back bristled and he snarled to himself. But he said nothing to annoy the horse. The wolf hated all other creatures, but he was not going to fall out with one as big and as strong as the horse.

Instead the crafty wolf tried to think of some way of making himself agreeable to the horse. Out of the corner of his eye he saw the field of oats waving in the wind.

"Look at that fine field of oats over there," he said. "I saw you coming and I know horses like eating oats, so I left them all for you. Wasn't that kind of me?"

"You don't fool me," grunted the horse, not at all impressed. "I know that wolves don't eat oats. If you did they would all be gone by now."

| Moral | *There is no virtue in giving someone something we do not want ourselves.* |
|-------|------|

# THE TREES AND THE AXE

A woodman went into a forest. The great trees surrounded him. They were tall and thick and strong. Most of them had been in the forest for hundreds of years.

"I am sorry to disturb you," said the woodman politely, "but I can see that you great trees are the kings of the forest. I have a request to make. I need wood to make a new handle for my axe. I wonder if I could cut down a tree for this purpose. I don't mean one of you, of course, just a small tree somewhere."

The great trees were flattered at being spoken to in this manner and nodded their heads graciously.

"You do not ask for much," they said. "Yes, you may take just one small tree. You may cut down that young sapling over there."

The older trees nodded at a young ash tree which had not had time to grow very tall or thick.

The woodman thanked them for their kindness. He walked over to the ash tree before the older trees could change their minds. With a few swift strokes he cut down the ash tree. Then he sat down and made a fine new handle for his axe from the fallen tree.

As soon as his axe had been repaired, the woodman showed the old trees the real reason for his arrival. Wielding his strong, new axe, he cut down every tree that stood in his path. He went right through the forest, hacking and cutting at all the trees he could find, big and small alike.

Before long most of the forest had been cut down. The few surviving trees, who once had welcomed the woodman into their midst, wailed in despair and sorrow.

"It is our own fault," they cried. "We have brought our deaths upon ourselves. We should not have stood by and let the woodman cut down that first tree. If we had protected that sapling we would have been guarding ourselves."

| **Moral** | *Unity is strength.* |

# THE EAGLE AND THE BEETLE

The eagle and a tiny beetle fell out with one another and became deadly enemies.

It happened like this. One day the eagle was chasing a hare across a field. It swooped low over the terrified animal, its great claws extended, its beak ready to strike.

The poor hare ran as fast as it could, screaming for help. The only living thing it could see was the tiny beetle.

"Help me, beetle! Please help me!" cried the hare piteously.

The beetle was small but brave. "Eagle!" he cried in his loudest voice. "I am speaking to you, Eagle! Do not touch that hare. It is under my special protection!"

Of course, the eagle took no notice at all. In fact he hardly noticed the tiny beetle. Suddenly he pounced upon the hare and ate it.

The beetle was very upset about this and decided to avenge the hare.

He made his way to the eagle's nest, high in the cliffs, and waited. Then, every time that the eagle laid an egg, the beetle rolled it out of the nest, so that it fell to the ground below and was smashed.

The beetle destroyed so many eggs in this way that the worried eagle went to the god Jupiter, and asked his advice.

"You may lay your eggs in my lap," said the god. "They will be safe there. The beetle will not dare approach me."

But Jupiter did not know how determined the tiny beetle was. When he started something, the beetle always did his best to finish it. He waited until

the eagle had laid a clutch of eggs in the god's lap. Then he rolled a lump of earth into Jupiter's lap.

When the god saw the dirt on his lap he stood up quickly and brushed it off. But he had forgotten that the eagle's eggs were also on his lap. As he stood up, these fell to the ground and were smashed. The beetle had won again!

Since that day, or so it is said, eagles have always made sure that their eggs are laid in a safe place, which is why people hardly ever see them.

| Moral | *Great determination can overcome most odds.* |

# THE GOATHERD AND THE GOAT

Soon night would be falling. The goatherd wandered anxiously over the side of the mountain, rounding up all the goats in his charge. He had to get them all back to their pen at the farmhouse before it grew dark.

One by one the goats came to him as he called and whistled. The goatherd counted the goats. There was no doubt about it, one was still missing.

The man looked about him. To his relief he saw the missing goat in the distance. He shouted to the animal to come to him. The goat paid no attention.

Again and again the goatherd shouted and whistled. It was to no avail. The goat would not approach him. The man began to grow desperate. If he returned to the farm with one goat missing, the farmer would blame him.

Losing his temper, the goatherd picked up a stone and threw it at the animal. He did not mean to hurt it, but as it happened, the stone hit the goat on the head and broke the tip from one of its horns.

"Oh dear!" cried the goatherd, running towards the goat. "Please don't tell the farmer what I have done to your horn."

"You silly fellow," bleated the goat. "Can't you see that my broken horn will show what you have done to me, even if I don't tell the farmer?"

| Moral | It is no use trying to hide what cannot be hidden. |

# A WOLF IN SHEEP'S CLOTHING

"There are dozens of sheep in that flock down there," said a wicked old wolf to himself, gazing down at a field. "How can I get close to them so that I can kill and eat some?"

Then he had an idea. He found an old sheepskin and wrapped himself up in it, so that he looked like a sheep. Then he walked down to the field and joined the flock of sheep grazing there.

The sheep thought that the wolf was one of them, so they paid no attention to him as he moved among them. Not even the shepherd noticed who the wolf really was.

The wolf decided that it would be best to wait until dark before he pounced on the fattest sheep and ate it. By that time the shepherd would have gone home.

When the sun went down behind the distant hills, the shepherd drove his sheep and the wolf in the old sheepskin into the pen which gave them shelter at night. Then he went off to his cottage to sleep.

The wolf had just decided which sheep he was going to leap upon, when suddenly the door of the pen was thrown open. A farmer stood in the doorway.

"We want some fresh meat at the farmhouse," he said. "One of you sheep will do. Yes, you over there! You look like a big fellow."

With that, the farmer lifted his axe and brought it crashing down on the wolf, thinking that he was a sheep.

| Moral | *Sometimes we can be too clever for our own good.* |
|---|---|

# THE SOLDIER AND HIS HORSE

Long ago there was a soldier who took great care of his horse. He knew that in battle his life might depend upon his steed. He always made sure that his mount was fed upon the best oats. He always gave him the cleanest water to drink. He made sure that his grooms polished the horse's sides until they shone. At night the soldier would never sleep, until he was sure that his horse was well-cared for and had a roof over its head.

In return the horse served its master well. It carried the soldier into battle and never flinched or turned away, no matter how fierce the fighting.

But then the war ended and the soldier rode back home. He put away his sword and his armour and became a farmer. He spent his days working in the fields.

In its turn the horse was also set to work on the farm. From dawn to dusk it toiled in the fields. It pulled a plough and did all the other hard jobs on the estates of its master.

Because there was no more fighting to be done, the soldier, who was now a farmer, no longer paid any attention to his steed. The horse was fed upon the poorest chaff. No one polished its coat and no one seemed to care where it slept at night.

Because of this neglect the horse grew thin and miserable. It was now a work-horse, not a warhorse.

Then one day the war broke out again. The farmer was asked to become a soldier once more. He answered his call. He put on his armour, took up his sword and gave orders that his horse should be brought in from the fields, its coat polished and its saddle put back on.

All this was done, and the soldier set off on his mount. He did not get very far. The years of neglect had made his horse thin and weak. It could not carry the weight of its master. Before long its knees buckled and it fell to the ground.

"You will have to travel on foot," it told the soldier. "Years of hard work and bad food have turned me from a horse into a donkey. You cannot turn a donkey back into a horse at a moment's notice."

| Moral | *We must treat people properly if we expect their help.* |
| --- | --- |

# JUPITER AND THE MONKEY

There was great excitement among the animals. The god Jupiter was going to give a prize to the animal who had the most beautiful baby.

Animals from all over the jungle gathered in a huge group. They came from the hills and the valleys, the plains and the rivers. They all brought their babies with them to be judged.

With a great fanfare of trumpets, the god Jupiter arrived among them, coming down from the skies. He walked among the hundreds of animals, looking at each baby very carefully before making up his mind.

One of the animals was a monkey, clutching her baby. Jupiter stopped and laughed when he saw the flat-nosed, hairless little creature.

"What on earth are you doing here?" he roared. "You have no chance of winning the prize. I have never seen such an odd-looking little creature in my life!"

The great god passed on. The monkey held her baby close to her.

"I don't care what Jupiter or anyone else thinks," she whispered. "To me you are the most beautiful baby in the world."

| Moral | *Beauty is in the eye of the beholder.* |

# A MAN AND HIS SONS

Once there was a man who had five sons. Instead of living together calmly and quietly, these sons were always quarrelling among themselves.

Their father grew tired of their constant bickering. He made up his mind to show them how silly they were.

He picked five sticks, each the same length, from the woodpile. Then he tied them together into a bundle. When this was done, he called his five sons to him. At first they did not hear him, because they were too busy arguing, but in the end they came.

"Listen to me!" shouted their father. "Take this bundle of sticks, and break it over your knee."

"I can do that easily," scoffed the eldest son.

He took the bundle and pulled it against his knee with all his force. No matter how hard he tried, he could not break the five sticks in the bundle.

"It can't be done," he growled at last.

"Of course it can," shouted his brothers. They all began arguing as to which of them should be the one to break the bundle. In the end they all tried in turn. Although their knees became sore, the bundle of sticks remained unbroken.

"Now let me show you how it can be done," said their father grimly.

He took the bundle of sticks from the others and untied the rope which held them together. Then he handed one stick to each of his five sons.

"Now, each of you break the stick in your hands," he ordered.

The sons did as they were told. Each stick cracked easily, like pieces of matchwood.

"What do you make of that?" their father asked them.

His sons looked puzzled, shrugging and making no answer. Their father sighed.

"Don't you see?" he explained patiently. "When a man stands alone, he can be broken as easily as one of those sticks. But when a man stands united with others nothing can break him."

Only then did his sons understand what their father had been trying to tell them, and they were all ashamed of themselves.

| Moral | *United we stand, divided we fall.* |

# THE OX AND THE FROGS

A family of frogs lived happily in the rushes of a pool. The two youngest frogs spent hours every day playing happily at the side of this pool. They made friends with all the other creatures living there and all the animals who came to drink the water.

One day, however, a dreadful accident took place. A great ox came lumbering down to the water's edge to drink. This beast was so big that he did not notice the two little frogs. As he made his way to the edge of the pool, he trod on one of them and squashed him flat.

Sadly, the remaining little frog went home and told his mother what had happened at the water's edge.

"A great big creature trod on my brother and killed him," he wailed.

"How big was this animal?" demanded his mother. She puffed out her cheeks and her sides. "Was he as big as this?" she asked.

"Oh, much, much bigger than that," replied the little frog.

The frog's mother puffed and puffed and puffed. She made herself as big and as round as a very fat pumpkin.

"Was he as big as. . . ." she began – but then she burst.

| Moral | *There are some things which it is better not to know.* |

# THE LAMP

The lamp was very proud of itself. It was polished and very beautiful. It was filled with oil and when it was lit, it shone so brightly, casting a soft, glowing light over the room it was in.

"Just look at me," said the lamp proudly. "I really am a most wonderful lamp. I give as much light as the silver moon in the sky. I shine as beautifully as the moon and all the stars in the heavens put together. More than that, I really believe that I shine as brightly as the great sun itself."

At that moment a great gust of wind blew into the room through the open window. The wind was so strong that it blew the light of the lamp out altogether. The room was plunged into darkness.

"Now do you see how foolish you are?" asked the lamp's owner as he relit the lamp. "How dare you compare yourself with the sun, moon and stars. They all cast their light for ever, while a mere puff of wind can put you out!"

| **Moral** | *Pride comes before a fall.* |

# THE TRAVELLER AND HIS DOG

A man was about to set out on a long journey. He was rather fussy and wanted everything to be just right. In order to make sure that this was so, he spent days getting ready. He tidied everything up in his house and prepared a great deal of food for the trip.

When he was quite ready, he put on his travelling clothes and put his pack on his back. Only then did he leave his house. His faithful dog was waiting for him outside.

"Why are you sitting there, doing nothing?" grumbled his owner. "Do I have to do everything? Come on, get ready to come with me."

The dog wagged his tail politely.

"But I am ready, Master," he said. "*I* have been waiting for *you*!"

| **Moral** | *We tend to blame others for our own mistakes.* |

# THE SPENDTHRIFT AND THE SWALLOW

A man came into a great fortune. Instead of putting some money by in a safe place for his old age, he set out to spend it all as quickly as he could. He became a spendthrift, someone who must buy everything he sees.

Before long, the foolish man had nothing left but the clothes he stood up in. He did not have a single coin left of all his fortune. Still, he was not worried. He believed that the future would take care of itself. Somehow he would be all right.

One day, as he was walking along a country road on a fine spring morning, he felt happy and lazy. The sun was shining and the air was warm.

As he ambled along the road without a care in the world, he glanced up into the sky. Swooping between the white clouds was a solitary bird.

"I do believe that's a swallow!" exclaimed the man with delight. "They only fly here when summer is on the way. There must be many other swallows coming. That means that summer is almost here."

The man thought that he had solved his problems. If summer was coming, he would not need his coat. He could sell it and buy food with the money.

He did just that, selling his fine coat to the first person he met on the road. But almost at once, things began to go wrong. The spring weather turned very cold, killing many birds and wild animals. The shivering man came across the swallow's frozen body on the ground.

"Because of you I sold my coat," he wailed. "Now I am freezing!"

| Moral | *One swallow does not make a summer.* |

110

# THE QUACK FROG

A frog grew bored with living by the banks of a pool and croaking all day long. He decided to move to the town and make his fortune. In order to do this, he thought he would set up a stall in the market place as a quack doctor. This is not a real doctor but a false one who claims to be able to cure anything.

So the frog hopped into the market-place and set up a stall. He filled the counter of this stall with all sorts and sizes of bottles. He had green bottles, blue bottles, brown bottles and clear ones.

When he was ready he climbed on to a box, so that all could see him, and began to shout.

"Roll up! Roll up!" he cried. "Come to me with all that ails you, and I promise to cure you of all illnesses!"

A great crowd of animals, attracted by this rash promise, began to gather about the frog's stall. Among the onlookers was a fox.

"Are you sure that you can cure anything?" asked the fox.

"Of course," lied the frog. "I have studied with the most famous doctors in the world. The contents of my bottles can cure all ailments."

At these words the animals began to press forward, buying the bottles from the frog at a great rate. But the clever fox was not satisfied. After looking on for some time he asked quietly, "If you are such a clever doctor, how is it that you cannot walk, only jump? And why is your skin so blotchy and wrinkled?"

There was no answer to this. The crowd of animals began to shout and jeer and demand their money back. The frog was forced to hop away from the town back to his pool.

| Moral | *Physician heal yourself.* |

# THE PIPING FISHERMAN

A fisherman who was very good at playing the pipe, wanted to become a musician. He would much rather play the pipe than fish. Every day, however, he had to go down to the sea, throw his nets into the water and hope that they would fill with fish.

One day, he took his pipe with him when he went to work by the side of the rolling ocean.

"Everyone says that I make lovely music with my pipe," he said to himself. "Why don't I play to the fish? My music should attract them and make them come up on to the shore. Then I won't have to bother to throw my nets out."

This is just what he tried to do. The fishermen stood by the sea for hours, playing as well as he could upon his pipe. Not one fish jumped out of the water on to the beach.

In the end, muttering to himself, the disappointed fisherman put his pipe into his pocket and went back to his nets. He threw them into the sea. When he hauled them back in to the shore again they were full of fish.

"Why is it that when I piped not one of you would dance?" he demanded crossly. "But now that I have stopped piping, you are all dancing?"

| Moral | *In order to succeed we have to work, not play.* |

# THE NORTH WIND AND THE SUN

The North Wind and the Sun met far above the Earth and had a great argument.

"I am stronger than you!" roared the North Wind.

"Oh no, you're not!" smiled the Sun happily.

For weeks, their argument raged. Neither the Sun nor the North Wind would give way. They became so wrapped up in their dispute that they ignored their jobs. The North Wind did not blow, and the Sun would not shine.

In the end they decided that they must settle their argument once and for all, before something dreadful happened to the weather on Earth.

In the end they agreed that the first of them to separate a certain traveller from his cloak could consider himself the stronger of the two.

The North Wind tried first. He leapt upon the poor traveller, roaring and blowing. He tried his hardest to tear the cloak from the man's body. He failed.

All that he did was to make the windswept man hug his cloak closer to him for protection.

"It's impossible," groaned the North Wind, retiring and leaving the traveller to continue on his way. "If I can't separate that man from his cloak with all my strength, I'm sure that you won't be able to, Sun."

The Sun did not answer the surly North Wind. He merely carried on smiling. He smiled down on the traveller below him. His smile began to make the traveller feel warm. Before long, the man stopped hugging his cloak to him and let it fall open. The Sun's smile grew warmer and warmer. The traveller threw his cloak back behind him, so that it hung from his shoulders. Still the Sun smiled. The Earth grew warmer and warmer. Everything began to wilt and droop in the enormous heat. In the end, the traveller knew that he did not need his cloak at all. He took it off and trailed it in the dust behind him.

The Sun turned to the North Wind. He still said nothing, but his smile grew even wider.

| Moral | *It is sometimes possible to gain by persuasion what cannot be gained by force.* |
|-------|-----------------------------------------------------------------------------------|

# THE MICE AND THE WEASLES

For months the weasels and the mice had been at war. The weasels were bigger and stronger than the mice, they won battle after battle. The surviving mice called a meeting.

"I have a plan," said one mouse. "We have lost all our battles because we do not have any leaders. I vote that we choose four mice to be our generals and lead us into battle."

The other mice agreed that this was a good idea. They chose four mice to be generals to lead them in the war. To show that they were generals, the four mice were given large helmets with great feathers called plumes in them. They also had large heavy badges dangling on ribbons from their necks.

Before long, the four generals began to feel very important. They held many meetings at which they made plans to defeat the weasels. They talked so bravely it made them feel proud and strong.

When they felt that they were ready, they led the other mice into battle. Alas, for all their plans they were still defeated. After a fierce battle the mice turned and fled.

Most of the mice reached their holes and were safe. The four generals ran too, but they were so weighed down by their plumed helmets and badges that they were the last to reach their holes. When they did, their helmets and badges were so big and heavy, they could not get in quickly enough. The weasels caught up with the poor generals and fell upon them.

| Moral | *Vanity is foolishness.* |

# THE SWAN AND THE CROW

There was once a black crow who wanted to be a white swan. This crow lived in a tree, like all other crows. He led a perfectly happy life, with a strong nest to live in and good food to eat, but he was not content. He saw the graceful swans beating their way through the air with their strong wings and sailing proudly on rivers, and wanted to be just like one of them.

"I wish my wings and body were white like the swans are," he said to himself. "Why can't I be like a swan? It's just a case of trying hard enough."

So the crow decided to turn himself into a swan. First he went to live by the side of a river, as the swans did, leaving his warm nest in the tree. For weeks he watched the swans as they floated on the water and flew into the sky, trying to remember everything that they did. Then he set out to copy them in every detail.

He taught himself to swim in the flowing water. Each day he scrubbed away at his black feathers, trying to make them white. He ate the same food as the swans.

Nothing worked. The crow's body remained black. The swans' food did not agree with him and he grew thin. The water made his wings weak and bedraggled.

In the end, the crow realised that he was never going to turn himself into a swan. This disappointed him so much that he flew away from the river and died.

| Moral | *We may change our habits, but we cannot change our nature.* |

# THE FORTUNE TELLER

It was market day in the town. There were stalls everywhere, selling all sorts of goods. Standing in the middle of the crowd was a fortune teller. He was doing a great trade, taking coins from the men and women around him, and in return telling them what was going to happen to them in the future.

The people around him were hanging on to his every word. They said "Ooh!" and "Aah!" at each future foretold by the man in the centre of the crowd. More and more men and women joined the throng, crowding in on the fortune teller, all eager to find out what was going to happen to them in the future.

Suddenly a boy began to push his way through the crowd.

"Stand back there, lad," called out the fortune teller in a bad temper. "You cannot jump in front of the others. You must wait your turn to hear what the future holds for you."

"But I've come to tell you the news!" gasped the boy.

"What news?" frowned the fortune teller.

"Your house has been broken into!" cried the boy. "Thieves have stolen everything you own!"

"What did you say?" demanded the fortune teller, turning bright red with anger.

"Thieves have robbed you!" shouted the boy impatiently.

At once the fortune teller forgot why he was in the market square. He fought his way through the crowd and ran home.

The crowd stared after him in amazement.

"That's odd," said one of them. "He claimed to know what was going to happen to us, but he could not tell that his own house was going to be robbed!"

| Moral | *We should make sure that our own house is in order before we give advice to others.* |

# THE OAK AND THE REEDS

An oak tree grew by the river. It was a big tree and very proud of its size and strength.

"I am the biggest and strongest of all trees," he would cry loudly. "No one can bother me!"

Quite close to the oak tree, by the river bank, grew a clump of reeds. These reeds were quiet and shy, whispering softly as they swayed in the breeze.

One day a fierce wind blew across the land. It howled and roared. It tore the branches from trees and sent the roofs of houses spinning off.

The oak tree stood and faced the wind, daring it to do its worst. It had always been stronger than any wind.

But that day the wind was stronger than the oak. It tore the tree up by the roots and sent it crashing to the ground. The stricken oak fell among the clump of reeds. The reeds were still swaying from side to side, they did not seem bothered by the wind.

"I don't understand it," sobbed the oak. "How can someone as frail and slender as a reed escape the anger of the wind, while a strong tree has been torn up by the roots?"

"You were too stubborn," whispered the reeds. "You stood and fought the wind, although it was stronger than you were. We reeds knew that we were weak and frail, so we bent before the wind and let it pass harmlessly over our heads."

| Moral | Sometimes in order to survive it is better to give way. |
|-------|---------------------------------------------------------|

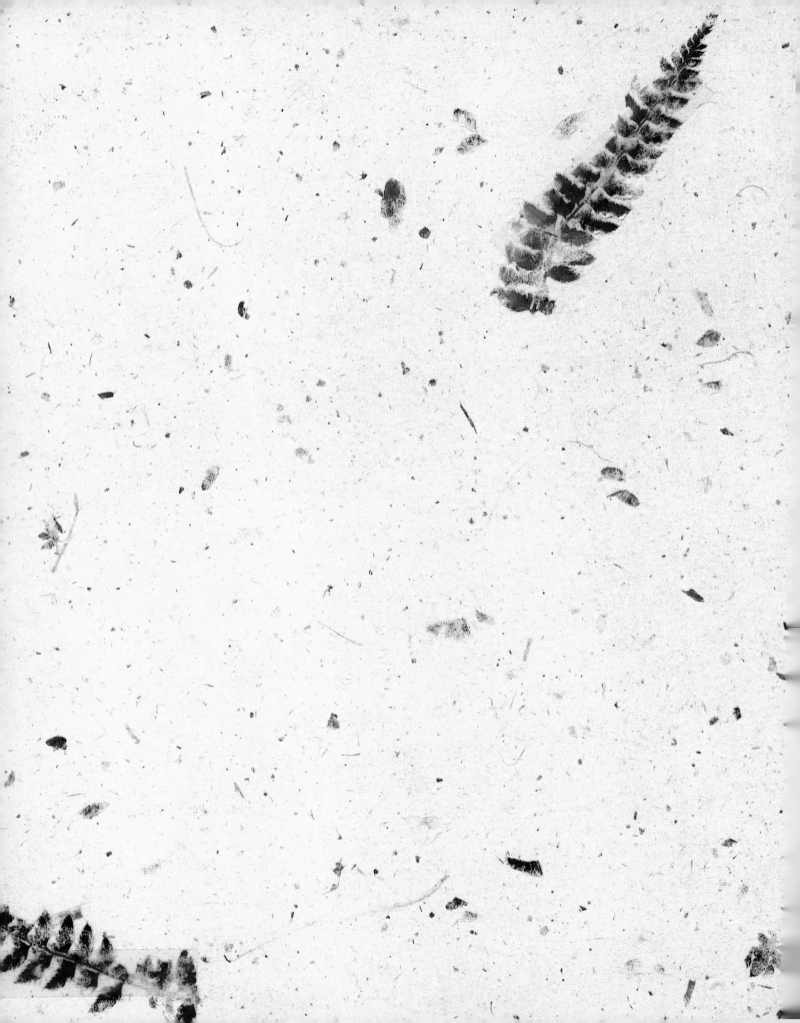